A BLUE for BEWARE

Jessie Haas
A BLUE for BEWARE

Pictures by Jos. A. Smith

 Greenwillow Books, New York

Text copyright © 1995 by Jessie Haas
Illustrations copyright © 1995 by Jos. A. Smith

Printed in the United States of America
First Edition
10 9 8 7 6 5 4

Library of Congress Cataloging-in-Publication Data

Haas, Jessie.
    A blue for Beware / by Jessie Haas ;
pictures by Jos. A. Smith.
        p.   cm.
    Summary: Lily and her friend Mandy compete against
each other in a horse show for the first time.
    ISBN 0-688-13678-8
    [1. Horses—Fiction.
2. Horse shows—Fiction.
3. Friendship—Fiction.]
I. Smith, Jos. A. (Joseph Anthony) (date), ill.
II. Title.
PZ7.H1129B1   1995
[Fic]—dc20
94-4572   CIP   AC

FOR MY FATHER,
BOB HAAS,
"THE MASTER"

CHAPTER ONE

THE SIGN POINTS toward the ball field behind the library. JUNIOR HORSE SHOW TODAY. Lily's stomach jumps, and she clutches the door handle of Gramp's big old truck. At last she is really here. The horse show is about to happen.

The truck creaks and rumbles onto the ball field. A cool gray mist hangs low. It makes the grass look very green. Other colors are bright, too: red bandages on a dapple gray horse; shiny blue, maroon, and silver trailers; the rusty brown snow fence ring that Gramp helped set up last night.

Gramp parks the truck. When the engine shuts off, Lily can hear Beware in the back, crunching hay.

"See Mandy anywhere?" Gramp asks. Lily is looking, as her fingers fumble at the seat belt. Nearby is a trailer that looks like Mandy's. Standing beside it is a chestnut horse that looks a little like Shane. But the horse's tail is braided, and so is his mane, in little short braids evenly spaced along his neck. Mandy doesn't know how to make those braids.

Gramp hops out of the truck. "Hey, *Woodie!*" somebody yells. Everywhere Gramp goes, somebody knows him.

Lily climbs down on her side of the truck. She can't bring Beware out until Gramp is through talking. Just for a minute there is nothing to do but look.

There are horses everywhere: tied to trailers; cloaked in bright blankets; being led somewhere; being groomed. All the horses look tall and beautiful.

There are kids in breeches and crisp white shirts. Kids in chaps and cowboy hats. Parents bundled up in sweaters, with thermoses of coffee. Parents in shorts and goose bumps.

Under a yellow striped tent near the ring, a crowd of kids and parents gathers. Mandy might be over there, signing up for classes, getting her number. Last year, Lily remembers, they stood in line together. They were sharing Lily's old pony, and right up to the last minute they couldn't decide who should ride in which class.

But if Mandy is there, Lily does not see her.

Thump! Beware stamps inside the truck.

"Guess the little mare wants out," Gramp says. In a moment Lily hears the chain on the tailgate rattle. She starts toward the back of the truck.

"Lily!"

Lily turns. A girl in white breeches and a dark coat and hat is coming toward her. The girl leads the braided chestnut horse. It's Mandy! But she looks so grown-up. She looks like a rider in a magazine, and Shane looks like a magazine show horse.

"Lily, you don't have your riding clothes on!" Mandy's eyes are very bright, and she seems to have even more freckles than usual.

"Mom and Gran are bringing them," Lily says. She can't stop looking at Shane's braids.

"Doesn't he look great?" Mandy says. Her teeth

are almost chattering, she is so excited. "My mother did it! From a book!"

"Oh," says Lily.

Beware's hooves thud inside the truck as Gramp turns her. Now he leads her down the ramp.

Beware's coat glows dark red. Her mane hangs long and black down the side of her neck. When Gramp led Beware into the truck half an hour ago, Lily thought her mane looked beautiful. Now it seems shaggy and messy.

Gramp ties Beware to the side of the truck. "Hi, Mandy," he says, and: "Lily, better not stand there like a bump on a log. You've got to get this horse ready!"

Now it's time to hurry. Lily brushes Beware all over, with the currycomb, the hard brush, the soft brush. When she brushes Beware's belly, Beware curves her neck around and scratches Lily's arm with her bristly upper lip. Beware loves to have her belly scratched.

But Lily doesn't have time. She gets out a soft piece of cloth that used to be Gramp's T-shirt. She polishes Beware with the cloth until her coat is sleek and bright. She combs Beware's mane and tail until every hair lies straight and separate.

"She looks beautiful," Mandy says. It's true, but does Beware look like a show horse?

While she works, Lily listens to the sounds of the horse show. Even though there are so many people and horses, it seems quiet. Everyone is grooming and getting ready. Nothing has started to happen yet.

Mom says, "Brr! Chilly morning." She has Lily's good riding clothes over her arm and a mug of coffee in her hand. Gran is with her, in a gingham dress and a sweater. She has brought a big picnic basket.

"It'll get hot later," says Gramp. "All set for a day with the horses, Gracie?"

Gran snorts. "I'm here to spend the day with Lily," she says.

"Better get dressed, Lily," Mom says. "Oh, Mandy, don't you look sharp!"

Lily takes her clothes into the back of the truck. In the dark corner she starts to take off her barn clothes. "I'll go sign Lily up for her classes," she hears Mom say, right outside the wall of the truck.

"No racing!" Gramp warns her. "Remember what we decided."

"*You* decided!" says Mom.

"Barbie, you know it's right," Gramp says. Lily hears Mom make a little sound that doesn't quite agree with him.

Lily doesn't agree with him, either. She wants to ride in every class, all day long. She wants to win as many ribbons as she can. But Gramp thinks the racing classes in the afternoon might teach Beware bad habits. And Gramp is the one who knows the most about horses.

Lily pulls on her breeches, and buttons her fresh white shirt. She slides her feet into her tight boots. She puts on the dark jacket that Mom used to ride in when she was Lily's age. The jacket makes Lily feel tall and straight, the way she should look on a horse.

She puts her helmet on. She feels like Mandy now. The tall black boots pinch a little, but they make a nice hard sound as Lily walks down the ramp.

"Looks good!" Gramp says. But Mandy is looking at her hair.

Lily's hair is too short to braid and too long to disappear under her hat. So is Mandy's. They have exactly the same haircut. But this morning Mandy's hair lies neat and soft on the back of her neck.

"Come over to our trailer and I'll give you a hairnet," Mandy says. "There were two in the package."

The hairnet makes Lily's hair feel heavy and together and special. When Mandy has helped her put it on, Lily looks at herself in the mirror of Mandy's pickup. Now she looks grown-up, too. The mirror can't show how she feels inside.

"Do you think we'll win blue ribbons this year?" Mandy asks. "I've never won a blue before."

"Me, either," says Lily. Last year the pony wouldn't let them win. But this year Lily feels sure she'll win blue ribbons. This year she has Beware.

And this year Mandy has Shane. He stands beside the trailer, his copper coat shining. His braids are pulled so tight they make little Vs all along his neck. Shane is a good horse, too—and there is only one blue ribbon in each class. If Shane wins it, then Beware can't.

"Thanks, Mandy," Lily says.

Mandy is staring across at Beware, and she jumps when Lily speaks. "Oh. Um, good luck."

Lily walks back across the wet grass. The sounds are getting quicker and sharper now. There is a loud, whispery noise from the announcer's tent, and then the loudspeaker voice says, "Testing. Testing. Can you hear me over there, Woodie?" Gramp waves his hat.

"Thank you," says the announcer. "And welcome to the thirty-third annual Bradford Junior Horse Show. Halter Class will be starting in about seven minutes, there's coffee and doughnuts at the food tent—and the sun is coming out!"

CHAPTER TWO

THERE IS STILL a gray mist in the air, but the sun shines through it. It tickles Lily's eyes.

Mom comes back with Lily's number—number sixty-two. She pins the cardboard circle onto Lily's sleeve. "There! You look wonderful!" she says. "And so does Beware."

"Better go on over," Gramp says. "Let the judge get a look at you, before the rest of 'em crowd in."

Lily unties Beware. She folds the lead rope in her hand, and she turns Beware around.

Beware's head goes up. She points her ears at the ring, and she steps forward eagerly. "Look, Gramp!" Lily says. "She wants to go!"

"Ayup," says Gramp. "She's ready to win some ribbons!"

Other people are heading toward the ring, too. They lead their horses in, and Lily follows.

In Halter Class the cleanest, sleekest, best-behaved horse will win. Maybe it will be Beware. Her coat is very shiny. Her mane hangs like a soft, floaty curtain. She walks quietly. She is interested in the other horses but not nervous. Lily looks at the judge, to see if she has noticed.

The judge stands in the middle of the ring. She is wearing a cool skirt and blouse, comfortable shoes, and a big shady hat. She carries a clipboard, and she is writing something on it. Maybe it is something about Beware.

The ring fills up with horses. Everyone in the show goes in Halter Class. Little kids with ponies. Eighteen-year-olds who are almost grown-ups. Don Rice, who rides Western, in his black hat and shiny purple shirt. Ginger Taylor, who always wins the Jumping Class. Mandy and Shane are there, too. Shane keeps crowding into Mandy.

When all the horses are in the ring, the announcer says, "Line up, please." People bring their horses to stand side by side, in a line that goes from one end of the ring to the other.

The judge walks down the line, looking at each horse. Then one by one people lead their horses down the line in front of everybody. They turn around and trot back to place. Some horses won't trot, and some won't walk. But they all look sleek and trim.

Mom and Gran watch from the fence right in front of Lily. But there is nothing to see right now except a lot of horses standing still. Gran folds her hands on top of the snow fence. They look fidgety, with nothing to make or fix or clean.

Mandy and Shane go down in front of the line. Shane trots both ways, but he looks beautiful.

Don Rice is next. His buckskin horse is very clean, and it walks and trots perfectly.

And now the judge is looking at Beware.

Lily stands straight at Beware's head. Her heart thumps hard. She watches as the judge runs a hand down Beware's neck and looks for dirt on her fingers.

The judge puts her hand under Beware's mane, and there *is* dirt there. She makes a check mark on her clipboard, and Lily's face gets hot.

The judge walks behind Beware, past her unbraided tail—another check. Beware turns her head to look back at the judge. "Okay," the judge says. "Walk her out, and trot her back."

Beware walks and trots right beside Lily. Lily never has to pull on the lead rope. But by the time she gets back to the line the judge has already moved on.

When the judge has looked at all the horses, she writes on her clipboard and hands it to the ringmaster. The ringmaster goes to the yellow tent. He comes back with six ribbons, and the announcer says, "Okay, here are the results for Halter Class. In sixth place—"

Lily's heart pounds. What if *she* wins sixth? Or fifth? But she doesn't. She keeps waiting, and listening. What if Mandy's name is called?

When Don Rice goes to get the blue ribbon, Lily can see Mandy standing beside Shane. This is not like last year. Then they were little kids, and they got a ribbon in every class. In Halter Class they get no ribbon at all.

At least *neither* of them got a ribbon, Lily thinks. They are still even. She makes a "too bad" face at Mandy, and Mandy makes one back. Then it's time to go saddle up.

CHAPTER THREE

Now everyone is hurrying. "Where's my girth?" somebody yells. "I can't *believe* I didn't bring my girth!" Mothers and fathers are running around, too. Everybody has lost something or messed something up.

Gramp is waiting at the truck, with Lily's saddle over his arm. "Good little mare," he says to Beware. "She did just what she's s'posed to."

"But we didn't win a ribbon," Lily says.

"*Pfft!*" Gramp settles the saddle on Beware's back. "Who wants a ribbon for housekeepin'? That's what Halter Class is—just washin' and dustin'!"

"And housekeeping doesn't matter at all, Linwood?"

Gramp whirls around. Gran is standing there. "Oh, boy, now I'm in trouble!" Gramp takes off his green hat and holds it over his heart. "Gracie, I didn't mean it! Just trying to cheer Lily up!"

Lily tightens the girth and listens to the sounds around her. "Ow, get off my foot!" somebody yells. A horse walks by with no bridle on. He wanders just ahead of his owner, snatching bites of grass. Gramp picks up an extra lead rope and goes to help.

Lily bridles Beware. Then she mounts and rides over to the ring. Beware is calm, but she is eager to move. It feels good to be on her back, crossing the ball field with other riders all around.

The next classes are Equitation classes. The rider, not the horse, is being judged. The little kids always ride first, and they are in the ring now.

Lily tries to tell who will win, but it's hard. One little girl sits straight and still. But when her pony turns in circles, she doesn't do anything. She just sits there, looking scared.

One pony bucks, and the boy falls off. The pony trots to the gate, and Gramp catches it and helps the boy back on. Lily sees him say something, and the boy laughs.

All the little kids get ribbons anyway. Then it's the Juniors' turn.

Lily follows Mandy into the ring. There are lots of Juniors. They all look good. Even Mandy sits molded in position, like Lily's plastic cowboy who fits perfectly on his plastic horse. Nothing can shake the cowboy loose. It doesn't look as if anything can shake Mandy, either.

Lily rides Beware around the ring, just walking. She tries to remember everything Gramp and Mom have taught her. Sit up straight. Heels down. Elbows at your sides. She passes Mom, standing by the snow fence, and Mom says quietly, "Smile."

That's right. You're supposed to smile, too. It shows the judge that riding is easy for you and that you are having a good time. Lily stretches her lips and looks at the judge. The judge is looking at the clipboard.

"And trot, please!" says the announcer. "Rising trot."

Rising trot means posting—rising out of the saddle at every other step. Lily could never post right on the pony, but on Beware it's easy. For a minute everything feels fine.

Then there are hoofbeats, getting loud behind her. Beware puts her ears back, as if she might kick. Two horses pass, one on each side, very close. Their hooves drum, and a cloud of dust rises. One horse cuts in front, and Beware has to dodge. Lily loses the rhythm of the posting. She is bumping along, just like on the pony.

"And walk, please. Walk."

Lily sits deeper, and Beware starts walking. A chestnut horse flashes past. It's Shane. He goes halfway around the ring before Mandy can make him walk.

Lily tries to settle into the saddle and ride right. Next they all will have to canter. That will be even harder.

"And canter, please!"

Horses grunt as their riders urge them on. Some start cantering fast, and some won't canter at all. Two horses trot fast ahead of Lily. Their riders kick them in the sides.

Beware just lifts into a canter, in the gentle rhythm that Lily knows well. If they were alone in a field, Lily would want to canter like this forever.

But other horses keep passing and cutting in front. It is noisy and dusty. Beware has to slow down, and speed up, and dodge. She doesn't feel smooth now, and Lily doesn't have time to think about riding well.

"Walk," says the announcer. Now they have to turn around and do it all again, going the other way. It is just the same, except that Shane runs away with Mandy.

At first Lily thinks Mandy is showing off, galloping fast past all the other horses. But she goes all the way around the ring, and when she passes again, Lily hears her saying, "Whoa, Shane!" Mandy's voice sounds shaky and scared. Lily is scared, too. Shane is going so fast he could crash into somebody. Lily is glad when Mandy gets him stopped.

Finally the announcer says, "Line up," and in a minute the ringmaster brings back the ribbons. Lily doesn't see how she could get a ribbon. Unless maybe the judge didn't see her bumping at the trot. Unless maybe she was riding beautifully all along, even when it didn't feel that way.

"In sixth place," the announcer says, and Lily's heart thumps anyway, "number eighty, Mandy Firestone riding Shane."

Mandy? But Shane ran away! Didn't the judge see that?

Mandy rides forward with a proud, surprised smile, and the judge puts the green ribbon on Shane's bridle. Lily listens. Fifth place, fourth place . . . Mandy got a ribbon. Maybe she will get one, too, in spite of everything.

But Ginger Taylor wins the blue, and Lily follows her out of the ring, with everybody else who didn't win.

CHAPTER FOUR

Now there is time to rest. Lily takes off Beware's saddle, to let her back get cool. She takes off the hard hat and Mom's jacket, and she wants to take off her boots, but they're too tight. She is starving, and Gramp buys her a hot dog.

"I packed sandwiches," says Gran.

"That's lunch," Gramp says. "This is breakfast."

Lily sits down to eat. Across the ball field she can see the heads of the Senior riders, circling in the ring. From the corner of her eye she can see Mandy beside her trailer, smiling and chattering just as if she de-served that ribbon.

"Beware took good care of you," Mom says.

"Yes," says Lily.

"And *I* thought you looked good."

But it is what the judge thinks that matters.

"Junior Pleasure Class next," the announcer says. "Juniors in the ring, please."

Pleasure Class is supposed to show that your horse is easy to ride, with nice manners and smooth gaits. *This* will be the class, Lily thinks. Beware is a pleasure to ride, and the judge will see that.

As Lily goes into the ring, Mandy rides up close to her. Mandy's eyes sparkle, and she is smiling. She doesn't say anything. She is waiting for something.

After a second Lily makes herself say it. "Congratulations."

As soon as she says it, Lily knows it doesn't sound right. Her voice comes out mean-sounding, and she doesn't want to be mean to Mandy.

But it is too late. Mandy flushes. "Good luck!" she says. Her voice sounds just the way Lily's did. She rides forward to say something to Ginger Taylor and leaves Lily staring at her back.

* * *

Pleasure Class goes the same way Equitation did.

Walking is okay. But as soon as trotting starts, there is too much to watch out for. Slow horses. Fast horses. Horses passing too close. Horses that want to kick. Beware's trot feels rough and jerky, not smooth the way it is at home.

And when cantering comes, and Shane runs away again, Beware tries to run with him. For a second it is a race, Shane and Beware side by side.

Then Lily slows Beware down. But Shane gallops twice around the ring before Mandy can stop him.

Finally it is time to line up. All Lily wants is to get out of the ring and take her hot jacket off. She will not get a ribbon—but if the judge could come home with her, if the judge could see Beware jump over the brook and canter up the hill and trot smoothly along the trail through the woods, *then* Beware would get a blue ribbon. *Then* the judge would see that Beware really is a pleasure. . . .

"Sixth place goes to number sixty-two," the announcer says. Lily waits for someone to move out of line and go get the green ribbon. She wishes the person would hurry.

"Number sixty-two?" the announcer says. "I can't read this name. . . ."

"Hey, that's you!" says the girl next to Lily. She points to the number on Lily's arm.

"Oh!" Lily rides forward, and Beware stops all by herself, right beside the judge. Beware has won lots of ribbons before this, and she knows just what to do. She stands quietly, and she lowers her head so the judge can put the green ribbon on her bridle.

The judge looks up and smiles. "Nice," she says. "Now you just need to relax."

Lily hangs the green ribbon on the side of the truck. Across the wide space it faces the green ribbon on Mandy's trailer. Lily looks from one to the other.

Gramp isn't happy, though. "She was better than any of 'em!" he says, and he feeds Beware a carrot. "You should have won, little mare."

"Linwood!" Gran says warningly.

"The judge said I need to relax," says Lily, and Gramp snorts.

"Relax! How can you relax in the middle of a

goldarned stampede? Tell them others to relax—or go home and learn how to ride!"

Lily is surprised that Gramp is mad. Last year, when Lily got upset, he told her that horse show ribbons didn't matter. "It's the horse that matters," he said then, "and having fun."

Last year Lily did have fun. And a couple of times the pony even did what she told him to do.

But last year she didn't have to ride against Mandy.

CHAPTER FIVE

"The winner in Western Pleasure, Don Rice," the announcer says. "Now, could we have a few people in the ring to help set up the trail course?"

Gramp goes, and some other men. They set up a little jump and a wooden platform, like a bridge, for the horses to walk over. They drape a sheepskin over a barrel, to look like a bear. They hang a raincoat on a post, and they set up another post with a mailbox on it.

Lily and Mandy ride over to the ring. They get there at the same time, and they stop side by side. But they don't say anything.

After a minute Gramp and Mandy's mother come over. Gramp says, "Congratulations," to Mandy, and Mandy's mother says, "Congrats!" to Lily. Lily and Mandy look at each other now, but they still don't say anything.

One by one the little kids ride around the trail course. Some of them look scared, alone in front of all those people. They sit frozen on their ponies. When the ponies do the wrong thing, the riders don't do anything to stop them.

Other kids aren't scared at all, and they try hard. They pull on the reins. They kick the ponies' sides. But the ponies keep on doing what they want to, whether the riders try or not.

"That's me!" says Mandy, pointing, as a pony backs away from the sheepskin. "That's what Shane's going to do." Lily can't think what to say, but she feels better that Mandy has spoken.

"You have to be firm with him," Mandy's mother says. "Don't let him get away with things."

But Gramp winks up at Mandy. "Don't know as I'd want a horse that'd walk straight up to a bear. Would you?" Mandy laughs.

The little kids get their ribbons, and now it's the Juniors' turn. Ginger Taylor goes first, and her horse does everything perfectly. Lily strokes Beware's neck as she watches.

At home Beware does all these things, too. She walks over bridges, and she stands still while Lily gets the mail out of the mailbox. She doesn't get scared when Lily puts on her rattly raincoat.

But Lily knows that Beware would not walk up to a bear. She would turn and run. She would get both of them safely away. If Beware thinks that sheepskin is really a bear, she will not get a ribbon in Trail Class.

The announcer calls Mandy's name. "Uh-oh!" Mandy says, and rides into the ring. Shane is supposed to walk, but he is already trotting. He trots right past the mailbox. Mandy has to turn around and come back. After she has opened the mailbox, Shane moves away, and Mandy leaves it open.

Shane leaps high over the jump. He snorts and sidesteps when Mandy tries to put on the raincoat, and he makes her drop it. He won't even go near the sheepskin. And every time Mandy tries to guide him down the middle of the platform, Shane swerves at the last minute and walks beside it. Finally the judge tells Mandy to give up.

When Mandy comes out of the ring, her face is red. Her eyes are glittery with tears. For a second tears prick Lily's eyes, too.

"He's being *awful!*" Mandy says as she goes past. Shane won't stop, even now.

Gramp steps in front of Shane and catches him by the rings of the bit. He gives the bit a little shake, and he makes Shane stand still. "There! You ain't a *bad* horse," Gramp tells Shane. "Just got speed on the brain. Taking him in Barrel Racing?" he asks Mandy.

"I don't think so." Mandy wipes her eyes.

"You ought to," Gramp says. "Might settle him down if he gets the chance to run." Gramp turns to talk to Mandy's mother.

Lily stares at him. Why is Gramp telling Mandy to go in Barrel Racing when he won't let *her*? Does he think Mandy is a better rider? Does he think Shane is a better horse?

But now the announcer is calling her name. Lily rides into the ring. She looks at the people standing by the fence. There is Gran in her gingham dress, and Mom, smiling. Lily looks away. She sits straight and still in the saddle, like a molded plastic rider.

Beware stands quietly while Lily opens and closes the mailbox. She trots up to the little jump and hops over it. She doesn't move while Lily puts on the raincoat.

"Good, Beware," Lily whispers. She doesn't care, now, that everyone is watching. She walks Beware toward the sheepskin. "It's not a bear," she tells Beware.

Beware's steps falter for a moment. She snorts at the sheepskin. But when Lily squeezes with her legs, telling Beware to go nearer, Beware does.

"Good girl!" The sheepskin was the hard part. As she heads toward the platform, Lily is thinking that Beware has done everything perfectly. Maybe this will be the class for a blue ribbon.

Beware walks up to the platform. She pricks her ears and looks down at it.

Then, quietly and carefully, she walks past it, on the grass.

A groan goes up from the people watching. Lily's face gets hot. She turns Beware around, and she comes back toward the platform. She makes her legs firm on Beware's sides, and she shortens the reins. She points Beware straight at the middle of the platform. "Walk!"

Beware gives a big sigh. She lowers her head, and she walks across the platform. Above the thud of her hooves on the wood, Lily hears clapping.

"She goes over bridges all the time!" Lily says, outside the ring. "She *never* does that!"

"Course not," says Gramp. "She's got more sense!" He rubs with the flat of his hand under Beware's forelock. "And she's got more sense than to walk on a piece of wood when there's safe ground right next to it."

"That was just a pretend bridge," Mom says, "and Beware didn't know she was supposed to pretend."

But Lily should have known. She should have expected Beware to walk beside the platform, and she should have been ready. Gramp turns to tell Don Rice's father how smart Beware is, and Lily knows it is true. But it doesn't make her feel better.

She leads Beware toward the truck, and she thinks, just for a moment, that horse shows are stupid.

CHAPTER SIX

Now it is lunchtime. Lily takes Beware's saddle
and bridle off and ties her on the shady side of the
truck. She gives Beware some hay, and Gramp brings
a bucket of water. Gran and Mom spread out a blan-
ket on the grass and open the picnic basket.

"Are you having a good time, Lily?" Mom asks.

Lily knows she should say yes. Mom and Gran and
Gramp have helped her come here. It isn't nice to
be ungrateful.

But it isn't nice to lie, either. Lily just nods, and
she takes a big bite of sandwich so she doesn't have
to say anything.

Gramp shoves her leg with the toe of his work

boot. "Relaxed yet?" he asks, and he gives Lily a twinkly look from under his hat brim.

Lily swallows her bite of sandwich. "How come you told Mandy to go in Barrel Racing when you won't let me?"

"Thought she might win," says Gramp. "Got a bet on with Pete Rice."

"Linwood!" says Gran. Gran doesn't always notice when Gramp is joking. She doesn't always think he should be joking.

Gramp squashes his hat back on his head, and he winks at Lily. When Lily doesn't wink back, he says, "Racing makes a horse hard to handle, and Beware's too good to spoil. That horse of Mandy's is spoiled already, so I figured it couldn't do any harm."

Mom asks, "How many classes do you have left, Lily?"

Lily counts, and there are only two: Costume, which is just for fun, and Jumping. All three morning classes where she thought she might win a blue ribbon are over. Lily had been looking forward to them for a long time, but they went by too fast.

Mom looks at the green ribbon, fluttering in the

breeze. Then she says, "Pop, you're right about Barrel Racing. But the Flag Race isn't that bad. Don't you think Lily could go in that?"

Lily tries to remember the Flag Race. That's the one with three coffee cans nailed to posts around the edge of the ring. Each can has a little flag in it. You ride in carrying a flag, stop at the first coffee can, drop your flag in and take the other flag out, and keep doing that all the way around. The fastest one wins.

"That can get pretty wild, too," Gramp says.

"But it doesn't have to be," says Mom. "You can just trot if you want. Beware has a nice fast trot, and she'll stop on a dime. She might do okay."

Gramp scratches under his hat, the way he does when he is thinking. The hat tips way over on the side of his head. He looks at Beware, and Beware turns away from the hay to look back at Gramp.

"All right," Gramp says. "I'd like to see that."

"Then after lunch," says Mom, "Lily and I will go enter."

Mom and Lily walk over to the announcer's tent. Now there are ribbons with long blue, red, and yellow streamers hanging up. These are for the show champions, the people who have won the most ribbons. Don Rice will get one, and so will Ginger Taylor. Last night in bed Lily thought that she and Beware might get one, too. Now she knows they won't.

Mom says, "I want to enter Lily and Beware in Flag Racing—"

"Hi, Lily," says Mandy, coming up behind them. "My mother says I can go in Barrel Racing."

"Oh. Good."

Mom turns to look at Lily and Mandy. "And Breakaway," she says. "I'm entering you both in Breakaway."

"Why?" Lily asks. She can't even remember what Breakaway is.

"Because you do it together," Mom says, "and because it's fun. I think it's high time you two had some fun at this show!"

After lunch everybody puts on a costume. There are tramps and ballerinas, pirates, and a cow. The cow is a horse with plastic horns on its head. The udder is made of an inflated rubber glove.

Lily is the Headless Horseman. She wears a big black cape tied over the top of her head. It is hot inside, and the eyehole in the front keeps shifting so she can't see.

Mandy is a foxhunter. She has a red velvet jacket of her mother's. Mandy's father has brought their dog Flutters down. Flutters is a beagle, but he looks sort of like a foxhound. Mandy has to walk, so she can lead Shane and Flutters. She is even hotter than Lily.

Everyone in Costume Class gets a purple ribbon. Mandy's ribbon is for Best Props. Lily's is for Scariest. Lily pokes her head out now, and she rides over to the truck to leave her ribbon and her cape. The next class is Jumping, and she doesn't know if she wants to ride in it or not.

CHAPTER SEVEN

Lily makes sure her girth is tight. She buckles on the hot helmet. She takes a drink of water, and she lets Beware have a swallow. Then she rides back to the ring, to watch the others jump.

The jumps are low, just a little higher than a horse's knee. Lily and Beware have jumped higher than that. But Lily has never jumped six jumps in a row before. She has never jumped with a lot of people watching. She tries saying to herself, I don't care! She tries saying, Horse shows are stupid! But her stomach just gets tighter and tighter as she watches the first horses go.

Ginger Taylor's horse jumps perfectly. But some horses knock the poles down, even though the jumps are low. And one horse is so tall he doesn't seem to notice them, way down there. He won't pick his feet up high enough, and his hooves clunk on every single pole.

Another horse stops suddenly. Everyone gasps. The rider flies over his head and lands on the other side of the jump. But she lands on her feet, smiles, and shrugs. Lily knows if Beware does that, *she* will not land on her feet. She smooths Beware's neck with her hand.

"I'm not going in this," Mandy says suddenly. "I'll get killed." She rides away toward the announcer's tent. Gramp scratches under his hat.

"She's prob'ly right," he says. Lily's stomach turns like a washcloth being wrung out.

"Next," the announcer says, "Lilian Gifford on Beware."

"Nice and easy," Gramp says. "Pretend they're logs on the trail." He slaps Beware on the rump. "Off you go!" And Lily rides to the gate.

The timekeeper stands there, holding his stopwatch. He smiles at Lily and looks down at his watch. Lily looks ahead at the jumps.

This class is judged on how many times the horse touches the poles, and it's judged on speed. Other people have cantered. But when the timekeeper says, "Go," Lily makes Beware trot. She wants to go more slowly, so she can stay in control. The jumps are all in front of her, white and blue and yellow striped poles. Now they look high and like a lot more than six.

Beware trots toward the first one. It seems smaller and smaller, the closer Lily gets to it.

Suddenly the jump disappears. Beware is hopping over it, easily and smoothly. She points her ears toward the next jump, and she trots a little faster. All of a sudden Lily's stomach feels fine.

The next jump is easy, too. Now Beware wants to canter, and Lily lets her—but slowly. They are all by themselves in the ring, and Beware's canter is as smooth as it would be at home. This is just like jumping logs on a trail—but more fun, because after this jump there is another, and another.

Lily rises in her stirrups when Beware jumps. Her

hands follow Beware's reaching head, so she never jerks on the reins. She sinks softly back into the saddle when Beware lands, and she looks ahead to the next jump. She knows she is riding beautifully, and she has a free, singing feeling inside.

Then the last jump is behind her. But Lily feels as if she's just gotten started. She wants to canter right around the ring and jump them all again. Instead she has to ride out through the gate.

The timekeeper clicks his watch and calls out the time. Behind him Lily hears clapping. She stops and leans forward to hug Beware's neck.

Beware is hot and sweating. Her big breaths move Lily in the saddle. She tosses her nose up and down. Beware would like more jumps, too.

"She looks pleased with herself!" Gran says, coming up to them. Gran hardly ever notices how a horse looks.

"Beautiful!" Mom says. Gramp grins so broadly his pipe falls out of his mouth, and he has to catch it.

And Lily can't stop smiling. She hardly listens, even when the winners are announced. Sixth. Fifth. Then—

"Fourth place, Lilian Gifford on Beware."

The judge looks hot and tired now. She is sipping lemonade. She pins the ribbon on Beware's bridle, and she looks up at Lily. "I wish I could have given you the blue," she says. "You both looked lovely. You were right to start out slowly, but—I'm sorry."

"That's okay," says Lily. She rides out of the ring with the white ribbon on Beware's bridle. She is glad the judge has finally noticed what a good horse Beware is. She is glad that in the judge's mind that white ribbon should be blue. But mostly she is glad because the jumping was so beautiful.

Lily doesn't watch the Seniors jump. She and Gramp lead Beware to the cool shade of the truck. Beware walks with her head low. She is tired and relaxed.

Lily takes off the saddle and bridle. She gives Beware a drink, a juicy carrot, and some hay. She scratches Beware's belly, and Beware curves herself around to scratch Lily back.

Gramp brings over a pail of water that has been warming in the sun. He and Lily take big soft sponges,

and they sponge Beware all over. Beware sighs because the water feels good. She crunches her hay
slowly.

"Does she know she's a good horse?" Lily asks.

"We're tellin' her right now," Gramp says.

CHAPTER EIGHT

BY THE TIME Gramp and Lily have made Beware comfortable, Barrel Racing has started.

"Let's get a lemonade and go watch," Gramp says. "She'll be all right by herself." Beware's eyes are half-closed now. She has stopped chewing.

Lily walks with Gramp to get a lemonade. She has a blister on her ankle. Her nice white shirt is smudged with dirt, and it sticks to her back. But she can still feel what it was like, going over the jumps on Beware.

Mandy waits with the other riders. Shane looks tired and cross. Mandy looks tired and scared. Lily hands up her lemonade, and Mandy takes a long pull through the straw.

"Why am I doing this?" she asks. "I'm gonna get killed!"

"No, you won't," says Gramp. He takes one of Mandy's hands, and he slides it way up the rein, closer to the bit. He squeezes his hand around Mandy's. "Tight, like this," he says. "Let your hands follow his head, but don't take 'em off this spot on the reins." He goes to the other side and moves Mandy's other hand up, too.

Lily watches the riders. They are all Western riders, and they look tough in their cowboy hats. Don Rice is here, with a long dark patch of sweat down the back of his purple shirt.

There are three barrels. The riders go around them in a cloverleaf pattern, as fast as they can, and then gallop out through the gate. Lily has seen pictures of barrel racers going so fast the horses look as if they'll tip over, so close to the barrels that the riders' knees almost brush.

Nobody here goes that fast or that close. The riders can't turn the horses tight enough. They go wide, sometimes halfway across the ring before the riders can swing them around. Their strides look rough, and their eyes look wild. They look wildest at the end, when they're galloping toward the gate. The riders yell and kick and flap their elbows. As each horse passes through the gate, the timekeeper clicks his stopwatch and calls out the time.

When Don Rice goes, his buckskin horse doesn't seem very fast to Lily. But Don gets closer to the barrels than anybody. Lily sees Gramp laughing with Mr. Rice. Maybe he wasn't joking. Maybe he did bet.

When the announcer calls Mandy's name, Gramp hurries back. Mandy's hands have slipped down the reins. Gramp puts them up where they belong. "Don't worry about turning tight," he says. "This horse is a streak of lightning. Turn anywhere inside of a quarter acre, and you might just win!"

"Good luck, Mandy!" Lily calls.

She goes to the fence with Gramp. Mandy looks scared, waiting at the gate. She looks funny, with her white shirt and her black hard hat, and Shane in braids. Lily grips the top of the snow fence as she waits.

"Go!"

Mandy thumps Shane with her heels, but she still has tight hold of the reins. Shane leaps. He wants to run away, but Mandy won't let him. He gallops with his feet rising high in the air and swoops around the first barrel—wide, but not too wide. Now he is galloping straight toward Lily. Mandy has an amazed look on her face.

They turn around the second barrel, closer. Lily can see how hard Mandy has to pull. The third barrel. Shane looks crazy. All the way around—

Mandy points Shane straight toward the gate and loosens the reins.

"Go!" yells Gramp. He waves his hat in the air.

Lily yells, "Go-go-go!"

Shane flattens out and streaks like a rocket through the gate. He doesn't slow down outside the ring. He gallops all the way across the ball field in a perfectly straight line. People yell and dive out of the way.

The timekeeper says something, but Lily doesn't hear. She can't look away until she sees Shane stop at the far edge of the field. Mandy is okay.

"That's the best time yet!" Gramp says. He and Lily and Mandy's mother go out to meet Mandy, coming back. Shane is prancing and trying to run away again, but Mandy won't let him. Her hands are firm on the reins. She has a great big grin on her face.

"I did it!" she says. "I turned him! He didn't run away!"

"What do you call that race across the field?" her mother asks. But she is smiling, too.

"Well, he did run away then, but that's because I let him." Mandy gets off. Shane has white foam on his chest and neck. "I don't want to go in the Flag Race," Mandy says. She rubs Shane's ear. "He needs a rest."

"Hey, I think they want you back in the ring," says Gramp.

"Did I win a ribbon?" Mandy leads Shane through the crowd of horses into the ring. The judge is waiting, with a blue ribbon in her hand.

CHAPTER NINE

W HEN MANDY GETS her blue ribbon, first she cries. Then, with tears on her cheeks, she laughs. She hugs the judge. She hugs Gramp. She hugs Shane. Then she tries to hug Lily, and Lily holds her away.

"No! You're covered with horse sweat."

Mandy looks down at herself, and she laughs again. "I can't believe it!" she says. "I can't believe it!"

"Course, you need some lessons with this animal," Gramp tells her. "You shouldn't have to hold him that hard."

"I know," says Mandy. "But I *can* hold him. I found out that I can." She and her mother lead Shane away. The blue ribbon gleams on his bridle.

Gramp and Lily go to saddle Beware again. Beware has had a nice nap. She nickers at Gramp and Lily.

"You look all fresh and bright," Gramp tells her. He brushes Beware with the soft brush and puts more fly spray on. Then Lily puts on the saddle.

When she turns to get the bridle, Lily sees Mandy and her mother washing Shane. Finally Shane is standing still. The blue ribbon hangs above him on the trailer. Mandy and Shane deserve that ribbon.

Lily looks at her white ribbon for jumping. Nothing can take the happiness of jumping away from her. She still feels it inside her, like an open window with a breeze blowing through.

But Beware should have a blue ribbon, too. Beware has been good all day, and the good horses are supposed to win the blue ribbons. That's what Lily always thought, anyway.

She puts Beware's bridle on, and she rides over to the ring again. Gramp walks beside her. Beware will be the last horse. There is plenty of time to sit and watch.

Mostly these are the same riders who went in Barrel Racing. Their horses are lathered and wild-eyed, hard to stop. They charge past the coffee cans. They turn in circles while the riders are trying to change flags. One rider misses the can and drops the flag on the ground. He has to get off and pick it up and try again. Everyone, Lily thinks, is trying to go too fast.

Beware is watching, too. Her ears point toward the ring. She is tired and relaxed. But Lily can tell that she is still ready to go.

"You're such a *good* horse, Beware," Lily whispers. "You're going to have a blue ribbon, too!"

Finally the announcer calls Lily's name. "Remember," Gramp says, "just trot! I don't want you running this horse out the gate."

Lily nods. She will do just what Gramp says. But maybe Gramp doesn't know how fast Beware can trot.

At the gate the timekeeper gives Lily the flag. It is a little triangle of pink cloth, stapled to a stick. "Ready?" the timekeeper asks, and Lily nods.

"Go," says the timekeeper, and he clicks his stopwatch.

Lily trots into the ring, just the way she did in Jumping. Beware's trot is smooth and fast. She points her ears at the first coffee can. It looks like the can Lily brings her grain in.

Beside the coffee can Lily says, "Whoa." She sits deep and soft in the saddle, and Beware stops. She is so close to the can that Lily doesn't even have to stretch to reach it. Beware reaches her nose toward the can, but Lily tightens one rein and turns her head away. She puts the pink flag in, she takes the blue flag out, and she tells Beware, "Trot." Faster now, because Beware is so easy to stop. "Whoa." Blue flag in, green flag out. "Trot."

There is one can left. Beware trots toward it. It doesn't seem as if she is going fast because she is so calm and smooth. Lily can't tell; maybe they won't get a blue ribbon this time, either. But she knows they're doing well. . . .

"Whoa." Clunk, the green flag lands in the coffee can. Lily picks out the yellow flag.

Now! She clucks with her tongue, she presses her legs into Beware's sides, and she keeps a light feel on the reins, so Beware doesn't start cantering. Beware trots, straight and swift, toward the gate. Her ears are

forward, and her step is light. Through the gate—
Lily sits deep, and within two strides Beware stops.

Lily turns in the saddle as the timekeeper calls out
the time. He sounds surprised. After a second she
hears a whoop, and Gramp's green hat goes flying
through the air.

"That was the blue-ribbon ride!" the announcer
says, "Lilian Gifford, on Beware!"

"But it was *easy!*" Lily says, while the judge pins
the ribbon on Beware's bridle. "It was so easy!"

"It's supposed to be easy," says the judge. She
smiles up at Lily. "Everything at a horse show is easy
when you're good enough."

Jumping was easy, Lily thinks. And Trail Class was
almost easy.

"Thank you," she says.

"Do you think you'll do more jumping with this
horse?"

"Yes!" says Lily.

"Then maybe I'll see you again somewhere," the
judge says, and she turns away to give Don Rice his
second-place ribbon.

CHAPTER TEN

B REAKAWAY is the last class of the day. Before going into the ring, Lily rides over to the truck. She hangs her blue ribbon beside the white and green ones. It sparkles in the sun, and across the way, Mandy's blue ribbon sparkles back.

"Last call for Breakaway!" The announcer's voice floats across the ball field, and Lily turns to go. For the first time ever, her behind hurts from riding. She will be glad when it's time to stop.

Mandy is waiting in the ring, and beside her stands the ringmaster with a strip of blue crepe paper in his hand. He gives one end to Lily and the other end to Mandy. The announcer explains the rules.

"In this class," the announcer says, "you'll ride side by side, holding on to the paper. You'll walk, trot, canter, and turn around—and any other fiendish thing we can think of! If your paper rips, go into the middle of the ring, and wait. The last pair left wins. Everybody set? All right, then, walk."

Lily and Mandy hold their hands out toward each other, so close their knuckles almost touch. When they start walking, their knees brush together. "This isn't going to work," Mandy says, and she laughs.

Breakaway feels different from all the other classes. There are lots of riders in the ring—Juniors and Seniors, English and Western and ponies. But it doesn't seem crowded because everybody is riding two by two. Everybody is laughing. Nobody cares about winning Breakaway, but nobody's paper breaks at the walk.

"Trot!" says the announcer. Lily looks at Mandy, and Mandy looks at Lily. "Trot," they both say to their horses. Mandy takes tight hold of Shane, and Lily lets the reins float softly between her hand and Beware's mouth. They trot slowly side by side. Their knees stay close together, and the paper doesn't even stretch.

But right in front of them, two people do break their paper. One horse goes fast; one horse goes slow—rip! The riders groan, and laugh, and ride into the middle. There are other groans, and shouts, and whistles. The people watching at the fence are making a lot of noise. Lily sees Mom and Mandy's mother laughing together.

There are lots of riders in the middle now, but there are still lots left. "Canter, please," says the announcer.

This is where *their* paper will break, Lily knows. Riding one-handed, Mandy will never be able to keep Shane from running away.

Mandy thinks the same thing. "Here goes nothing!" she says to Lily, and they both canter.

Maybe Shane is tired. Maybe he has just learned that Mandy can stop him. Whatever the reason, he canters quietly, right beside Beware. There are more shouts and laughs, more people in the middle when the announcer says, "Walk.

"And reverse, please."

This is harder. Beware has to turn in a tiny circle, and Shane has to walk faster, in a big circle. The crepe paper stretches. "Whoa, Beware," says Lily. Beware stops, just for a second, and Lily and Mandy lean way out of their saddles, toward each other. Then Shane finishes his big circle. "Walk," says Lily, and they are going side by side again.

"There are only five left," whispers Mandy. "We'll get ribbons!"

Don Rice and his girlfriend are one of the pairs. Two little kids on ponies are still going, too—

"Reverse again," says the announcer, laughing. This time Shane makes the little circle, and Beware makes the big circle on the outside. The ponies get mixed up. As Lily turns, she sees them standing head to head. The little kids are way up on the ponies' necks. The crepe paper is stretched tight over the tops of the ponies' heads. But it isn't broken. When the little kids get themselves straightened out, everybody cheers.

"And trot."

This time Mandy and Lily forget to look at each other. Shane starts trotting fast, and Beware starts more slowly. The paper stretches, and Lily hears

Gramp shouting from the fence. Then it tears. Mandy trots ahead, waving a blue streamer.

Lily gives Beware a quick squeeze with her legs. She catches up as Mandy is turning toward the middle of the ring, and she reaches for Mandy's hand. "Hey, Mandy!"

Mandy looks back. She drops the blue paper ribbon and grabs Lily's hand. The paper was weak, but Mandy's and Lily's hands hold together strongly.

They look at each other. Lily can't tell which of them thinks of it first, but all at once they are holding their clasped hands over their heads, just as if they were the winners. They keep on trotting, all the way around the ring until they find a place to stand.

People laugh and clap. Gramp takes off his hat to them, and Mom gives a double thumbs-up.

Mandy and Lily's hands are stuck together with sweat. They make a little sound when they come apart—*schwuck!* Mandy and Lily laugh, and watch, while the announcer makes it harder and harder. Finally the little kids on the ponies are the only ones left. And then the horse show is over.

Gran has Band-Aids in her big square purse. She puts them on Lily's blistered ankles. "Well!" she says. "I've had all the horse *I* can stand for one day!"

Gramp leads Beware up the ramp. Lily can hear him inside the truck, talking to her. "Good little mare," he says. "You did a good job today."

Mom takes the ribbons down and gives them to Lily. "Did you have a good day?" she asks.

The big springs creak as Gramp puts the ramp up. Beware's hooves thud on the truck floor. Across the way Mandy is leading Shane into the trailer. She looks over at Lily and waves.

"Yes," says Lily. "I had a good day." She picks up the two best ribbons: the white one for jumping and the blue. Maybe she will hang these in the barn, where Beware can see them.

And the yellow one, for Breakaway, will go on her wall, right beside Mandy's picture.